Disney
5-MINUTE STORIES
STARRING
MINNIE

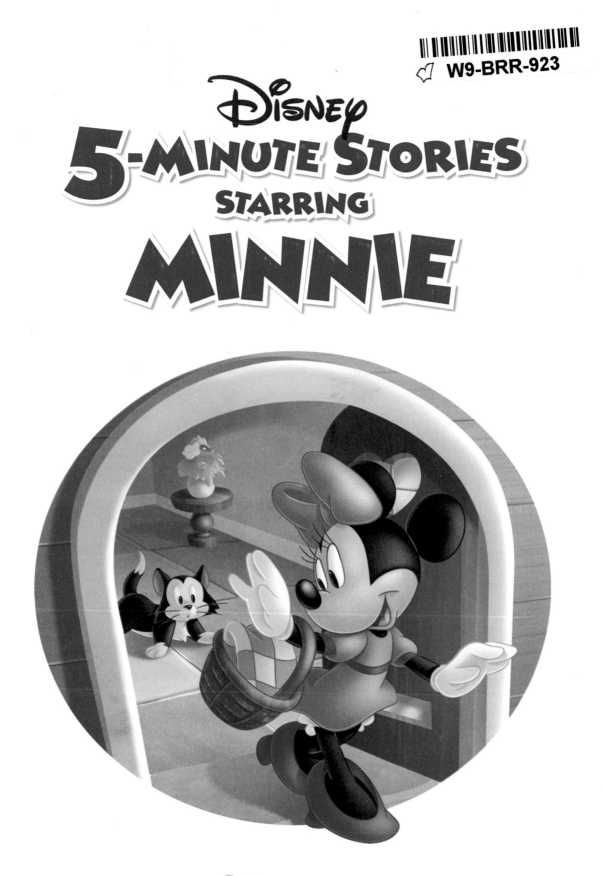

Disney PRESS
Los Angeles • New York

All illustrations by the Disney Storybook Art Team
Published by Disney Press, an imprint of Disney Book Group.
No part of this book may be reproduced or transmitted in any form or by any means, electronic or
mechanical, including photocopying, recording, or by any information storage and retrieval system,
without written permission from the publisher.
For information address Disney Press, 1200 Grand Central Avenue, Glendale, California 91201.
This special edition was printed for Kohl's Department Stores, Inc.
(for distribution on behalf of Kohl's Cares, LLC, its wholly owned subsidiary),
by Disney Press, an imprint of Disney Book Group, Los Angeles/New York.

Kohl's
Style Number 9781368043113
Factory Number 131635
06/18-08/18

Printed in the United States of America

First Hardcover Edition, August 2018
1 3 5 7 9 10 8 6 4 2
FAC-131635-18222
ISBN 978-1-368-04311-3

For more Disney Press fun, visit disneybooks.com

CONTENTS

MINNIE'S CAMPOUT

Mickey Mouse and his friends were excited. It was time for their annual campout!

Everyone had an important job. Mickey packed the tents. Goofy learned how to build a fire. Minnie and Daisy made dinner. And Donald bought some new flashlights.

"Is everybody ready?" Mickey asked when they had packed up the car. "Let's go!"

Mickey drove up a mountain and through the woods. Finally, he parked the car next to a lake. "Here we are!" he said.

"Gosh, smell that fresh air!" Goofy said as he took a deep breath. "What should we do first?"

"Let's set up our tents," Mickey suggested.

"I've never put up a tent before," Minnie said.

"It's easy!" Mickey told her. "Just slip the tent poles into the pockets."

"Um, Mickey?" Daisy said. "Where are the poles?"

Mickey's eyes grew wide. "Oh, no!" he exclaimed. "I forgot them!"

"That's okay, Mickey," Goofy said. "We'll have just as much fun sleeping under the stars."

As the sun started to set, Daisy shivered. "It's getting a little chilly," she said.

"Maybe we should build a campfire," Donald suggested.

"Sure!" Goofy replied. "Let's go find some firewood."

Mickey and his friends hiked into the forest to gather some firewood. When they had enough, Goofy showed them how to pile the sticks inside a circle of rocks.

"Stand back while I light the fire, everybody," Goofy said. Then he frowned. "Uh-oh. I forgot to bring the matches!"

"Don't worry, Goofy," Minnie said. "Our sleeping bags will keep us warm. Now, who's hungry? We have hot dogs, corn—"

"And s'mores for dessert!" added Daisy.

But Minnie and Daisy found a big surprise when they reached the picnic basket: the basket had tipped over, and something had eaten all the food!

"No tents, no campfire, and no dinner," grumbled Donald. "At least we have flashlights!"

Click.

Donald pushed the button on the flashlight, but it didn't shine.

Click.

He tried again. Nothing happened.

"Aw, shucks!" Donald cried. "I remembered to buy flashlights—but I forgot to buy batteries!"

Suddenly, a flash of lightning lit up the sky.

"Maybe we should just go home," Minnie said. "We can't camp in the rain without tents."

"Or dinner," added Daisy.

"Or a campfire," Goofy chimed in.

"Or a flashlight," Donald said.

Mickey agreed and the group rushed to the car.

No one spoke for the whole drive home. Mickey could tell that his friends were very disappointed.

As they walked into his house, Mickey had an idea. "I know!" he said. "Instead of having a campout, let's have a camp-in! We can camp right here in the living room."

"Oh, Mickey, what a great idea!" Minnie cried. "That sounds like so much fun!"

Mickey got the tent poles from the basement. Then he put up the
tents while Goofy built a fire in the fireplace.

Meanwhile, Donald found some extra batteries. In the kitchen, Minnie and Daisy made an even better picnic dinner.

Outside, the rain kept pouring down, but Mickey and his friends
didn't mind. Their tents were strong and sturdy. The fire was warm
and toasty. The flashlights shined brightly. And their picnic was
delicious!

SCAREDY-CAT SLEEPOVER

Minnie Mouse rolled her pretty pink suitcase up to her best friend Daisy Duck's front door. She and Daisy were having a sleepover! The door flew open before Minnie even had a chance to ring the bell.

"Hurry up!" cried Daisy. "I've got a ton of stuff planned for us to do!"

First, it was time for a fashion show. Daisy brought out makeup, jewelry, and some of her most glamorous clothes.

"We are going to look so cute!" Daisy said.

When they were done, Minnie looked at herself in the mirror. "I'm not so sure about cute," she said, laughing. "I think I accidentally made myself into a Christmas tree!"

Minnie decided that "Christmas tree" was probably not the next big fashion trend. So she and Daisy ditched their new looks and changed into pajamas. It was time to relax and enjoy a movie.

"My TV gets three hundred ninety-seven channels," said Daisy. "Let's see what looks good!"

They channel surfed until they came to a scary-movie marathon.

"Perfect!" Minnie said.

A movie called *The Invisible Monster with Ten-Foot Claws* was just beginning. Minnie and Daisy watched as an actress entered a spooky mansion. The door slammed behind her with a *BANG!*

"Eeek!" Minnie and Daisy jumped.

"You'll never get me, monster!" the actress cried. But soon she heard the *scratch, scratch, scratch* of the monster moving toward her.

The monster chased the actress all over the house.

Luckily, she managed to escape. But Minnie and Daisy watched the rest of the movie with the lights on.

When the movie was over, the friends got ready for bed.
Minnie tried not to jump every time she heard a strange sound.
Daisy tried to ignore the creepy shadows on the wall. Soon they
climbed into bed and wished each other sweet dreams.

But an hour later, they were still awake.

"That movie scared me," Minnie finally admitted. "Somehow
an invisible monster is even worse than one you can see. Just
imagining what it might look like gave me goose bumps!"

"I got goose bumps, too," replied Daisy. She tried to cheer
up her friend by making a joke. "Especially when that girl wore
the ugly sweater with mustard-yellow sparkles. I've never seen
anything so frightening!"

Minnie suggested they drink some warm milk to make themselves sleepy. After two big mugs full, they were back in bed . . . and still awake.

"It's not working," Daisy groaned. "What should we do now?"

"How about counting sheep?" Minnie replied. She closed her eyes and began picturing a meadow full of them.

Daisy closed her eyes, too, but she decided to count other things instead.

Finally, the girls started to drift off. Then, suddenly, they heard a loud *SCRATCH*!

"What was that?" Daisy cried.

"I don't know," Minnie said, huddling under her blanket. "Maybe it was just a branch scraping against the window?"

"Yes, that must be it," replied Daisy, but she wasn't convinced.

A few minutes later, they heard more scratching, and then a loud *SCREECH*!

"*Aaaahhh!*" yelled the girls.

"What if it's the Invisible Monster with Ten-Foot Claws?" asked Daisy.

Minnie took a deep breath. "Let's try to stay calm," she said. "I'm sure whatever is making those noises is perfectly harmless—and there's only one way to find out."

"What's that?" asked Daisy.

"We have to be like the girl in the movie and investigate," said Minnie.

"Okay." Daisy nodded nervously. "But I'm not dressing like her!"

So the pair tiptoed toward the sound of the scratching.
It seemed to be coming from outside the front door.

"Let's peek out the window," suggested Daisy. "Maybe we
can see something."

Minnie pulled aside the curtain and let out a loud gasp.

"What is it?" asked Daisy.

"Kittens!" cried Minnie.

She quickly threw open the door and brought them inside.

"Poor things. Do you think they're lost?" Daisy asked.

"Maybe," Minnie replied. "We'll ask around the neighborhood tomorrow and see if they belong to anyone."

"In the meantime, I'll make up the spare bed," said Daisy.

"What spare bed?" Minnie wondered.

Daisy grabbed her laundry basket. "This one!" she said.

"Who would have guessed that our monster would turn out to be furry and cute?" Minnie asked as she snuggled back into her bed.

"Not me!" Daisy replied, and the two girls burst into giggles.

Just a few minutes later, Minnie, Daisy, and the not-so-scary kittens were all fast asleep!

A PERFECT PICNIC

It was a beautiful spring day. Mickey, Minnie, and all their friends were going to have a picnic.

"Oh, Pluto," Mickey said as he packed Pluto's Frisbee, "this will be so much fun! We can all enjoy the sunshine together and share our favorite foods!"

Mickey packed a bone for Pluto's lunch.

Over at Minnie's house, things were not going so well. Minnie had packed all her favorite foods: a peanut butter sandwich, lemonade, and an apple. But as she got ready to leave, she started to wonder if she would like the lunches her friends had packed.

I don't want to share my lunch, she thought. *I want to eat it myself!*

Donald, Daisy, and Goofy felt the same way. They had all packed their favorite foods. But what if they didn't like what their friends had packed? Maybe it was better not to share lunches after all.

Mickey didn't know that his friends had changed their minds. Excited about their picnic, he filled his wagon and began to walk toward the park.

When he got there, he found his friends waiting for him. They all had baskets of food. But they didn't look very happy.

"What's wrong?" Mickey asked his friends.

"I don't want to share my lunch," Donald said.

"What if I don't like the lunch I get?" asked Minnie.

Daisy and Goofy agreed. Everyone wanted to eat their own favorite foods.

"Oh," Mickey said, disappointed. "I guess we don't *have* to share."

Minnie looked at Mickey. He looked so sad. She didn't want to be the reason he was upset!

Minnie handed Mickey her picnic basket. "It's okay, Mickey," she said. "I'll trade lunches with you. I'm sure I'll like whatever you packed."

"Really? Thanks, Minnie!" Mickey said.

Mickey's friends saw how happy Minnie had made Mickey.
They wanted to make Mickey happy, too.

"Will someone trade lunches with me?" Donald asked,
holding out his basket.

Daisy took Donald's lunch. Then she handed her basket to
Goofy, and he gave his basket to Donald.

Mickey laid out a blanket, and the friends got to

work setting up their picnic.

Minnie passed out plates.

Goofy handed out napkins.

Daisy gave everyone a cup.

And Donald set out forks.

Finally, it was time to eat!

Mickey opened his picnic basket first. When he saw what was inside, he started to laugh.

"What's so funny, Mickey?" Minnie asked. Then she looked in her basket and started to laugh, too.

Everyone had packed peanut butter sandwiches and lemonade!

The only difference in the baskets was the fruit.

Daisy had grapes.

Minnie had an orange.

Goofy had a banana.

Mickey had an apple.

And Donald had a pineapple!

"Isn't there some way we can share our fruit?" asked Minnie.

"I have an idea," said Mickey. "Leave it to me."

While his friends ate their sandwiches and drank their lemonade, Mickey cut up the fruit. He put it all in a bowl and mixed it together. Then he brought the bowl back over to the blanket. He had made a big fruit salad!

"What a great idea," Minnie said as Mickey passed out the fruit salad.

"Now we can all try each other's favorite fruits!" Daisy added.

Donald nodded. "Thanks for inviting us, Mickey," he said.

As Mickey's friends settled down to enjoy
the rest of their picnic, they realized that Mickey
had been right. Sharing *was* fun, after all!

THE BRAVEST DOG

It was a sunny day. Minnie Mouse was sunbathing in her backyard when she saw Mickey run out of his house and toward his car.

"Mickey, where are you going?" Minnie asked.

"Oh, Minnie, it's terrible," Mickey said. "A circus train was going through town and some of the animals got lost! The sheriff asked me to help find them before they cause trouble."

Mickey quickly climbed into his car. Pluto tried to follow, but Mickey stopped him. "You stay here with Minnie," he said, and drove away.

Mickey had not been gone long when Pluto began to tug at Minnie's skirt.

Minnie smiled. She knew exactly what Pluto wanted to do.

"Oh, all right, Pluto," she said. "It's not very likely that we'll run into any of the animals, and it is a nice day for a walk."

So Minnie followed Pluto down the path to the river.

Minnie and Pluto had not gone far when they heard a
hissing sound coming from behind a log.

"Eek!" Minnie cried. "Snakes! They must have escaped
from the circus train!"

But Pluto was not afraid of snakes. With a snarl, he
pounced into the grass . . . and found a small orange cat and
her six kittens.

"Oops," Minnie said with a giggle. "I guess it wasn't snakes
after all. Come on, Pluto, let's not disturb her."

Minnie stayed close to Pluto after that. If there were any loose snakes, she didn't want to run into them.

"It would be fun to find a bear cub, though," said Minnie. "Or a seal. I love seals! I wonder if one could come this far."

Suddenly, Minnie and Pluto heard a splashing sound coming from the river. Before Minnie could stop him, Pluto dashed down a hill and plunged into the cold water.

Minnie was right behind him. "Be careful, Pluto!" she cried.

But it was not a seal splashing around in the water. It was a little puppy who had fallen in!

Pluto laid the puppy at Minnie's feet.

"A cat and a puppy!" Minnie laughed, scratching Pluto behind the ears. "We'd better not tell anyone about our wild-animal hunting!"

"It's okay, Pluto," Minnie said as the two walked back to Mickey's house. "I love you even if you never capture anything wilder than a wet puppy."

Minnie turned to Pluto. "You know," she said, "what you need is a big bone! Why don't we go find one for you?"

But when Minnie and Pluto walked into Mickey's kitchen, they found that it was a disaster. Milk had been spilled all over the table, broken dishes littered the floor, and one of the windows was open!

"Oh, Pluto!" Minnie cried. "Someone has been in here! What if it was one of the circus animals? It could still be here. What should we do?"

Snarling, Pluto sniffed around the kitchen for a trail. Finally, with a loud bark, he leaped through the open window and raced across the yard to the woodshed.

"Be careful, Pluto," Minnie called. "Whatever it is may be dangerous!"

Just then, Mickey pulled up.

"Oh, Mickey," Minnie said, "something broke into your kitchen! Pluto is tracking it!"

Minnie pointed to the shed, where Pluto was slowly nosing through the door. As he disappeared inside, Minnie held her breath. What would Pluto find?

Long moments passed. Then, slowly, the shed door
opened again and Pluto came out. But he was not alone.
On his back was a tiny monkey dressed in a little hat and vest.

"Pluto, you did it!" Mickey said. "You found the last
missing circus animal!"

Mickey laughed as the monkey jumped into his arms. "Maybe this little guy isn't so wild after all," he said. "But it took a lot of courage to go into the woodshed after him."

"Pluto has been brave all day," Minnie told Mickey.

A few minutes later, Pluto was sitting beside the circus's ringmaster. He and Mickey had returned the monkey to him. "Thanks, Pluto," the ringmaster said. "The show couldn't have gone on without you!"

MINNIE'S SCAVENGER HUNT

One beautiful spring morning, Minnie woke up to find a surprise waiting for her. Someone had slipped an envelope under her front door!

"What could this be, Figaro?" Minnie asked. She opened the envelope and pulled out a note.

"Why, it's a secret scavenger hunt!" Minnie cried. "And look! The first item on the list is a picnic basket."

Minnie opened the closet and pulled out a soft blanket. She also took out a large basket.

"I can use this to carry everything," she said.

Placing the blanket in the basket, Minnie waved good-bye to Figaro and headed outside.

Minnie checked the list again. "Item number two: three cucumbers," she read.

Minnie knew just what to do. She went to her garden and chose several of the big, green vegetables. Adding them to her basket, she went to find the next item on her list.

"Hmmm . . ." said Minnie. "A stick as tall as I am. There's only one place to go for that!"

Minnie turned and was headed for the woods when she ran into Goofy.

"Hiya, Minnie," Goofy said. "What are you doing?"

Minnie was about to show Goofy her basket when she
remembered that the scavenger hunt was a secret. Then she
noticed that Goofy was hiding some blueberries behind his back.
Maybe he was part of the scavenger hunt, too!

"I'm just out for a walk," Minnie replied finally. "I'll see you
later, Goofy!" And with that, she hurried off into the woods.

Soon Minnie had found the third item on her list. In the distance, she heard rushing water.

"I wonder what that is," Minnie said, and she went to find out.

A few minutes later, she came upon a stream. Nearby was a patch of green plants with red peeking out from underneath. Minnie bent down to examine them.

"Strawberries!" she exclaimed. "These are the next item on my list!"

Minnie picked the strawberries and added them to her basket. The she checked her list again. The next item was five smooth stones. "Then stream is a great place to find smooth stones!" Minnie said.

Minnie left her basket on the shore and waded into the water. In no time she had found five smooth rocks on the streambed.

Minnie had only one item left on her list: a yellow flower. But as she looked around, she realized she was lost. She had wandered too far into the woods!

Minnie walked in one direction for a while, but somehow she just ended up back at the brook.

"Oh, no!" she said. "I'll never finish the scavenger hunt if I can't get out of the woods!"

Suddenly, Minnie spotted something on the ground.

"Blueberries! Goofy was picking these. Some must have fallen out of his bag," Minnie realized. "If I follow them, they should lead me back to the path and out of the woods!"

Minnie followed the trail over a log, through a bush, and under a heavy branch, until finally she found the path—and a patch of daffodils!

"A yellow flower!" Minnie cried. "That's the last item on my list!"

Minnie picked one of the flowers and added it to her basket. Then she happily skipped down the path. As she arrived at the park, Minnie saw her friends appear with their own baskets.